ANIMAL CRACKERS AND ALPHABET SOUP

Written by: Victoria Lovelace

AuthorHouse™
1663 Liberty Drive
Bloomington, IN 47403
www.authorhouse.com
Phone: 1-800-839-8640

Published by AuthorHouse 10/02/2012

ISBN: 978-1-4670-3532-3 (sc)

Library of Congress Control Number: 2011916707

authorHOUSE®

Dedication

Victoria Lovelace is dedicating her first book, "**ANIMAL CRACKERS AND ALPHABET SOUP**" to her amazing family. Victoria's husband Bobby has been very supportive throughout the creation of each alphabet story. They are blessed with awesome kids: twin girls, Lindsey and Mackenzie, as well as their older siblings, Jaydyn and Madisyn. Victoria thanks her family and her parents, Jim and Valerie Voll, for believing in her during this exciting journey!

Aa
ADMIRAL LEE

I **am an adorable army ant and** my name is **Admiral** Lee.
I live in **an anthill** beside **an ageless apple** tree.

The **apple** tree is near **a** swamp where **active alligators** like to swim **around and** play.
Sometimes, they swim **ashore and** fall **asleep** … they sleep **all** night **and** swim **all** day.

The swamp is near **a** forest **and among all** the trees **and** leaves **are affectionate antelopes, aardvarks, and apes.**
These **animals** live **around** the trees **and** munch on **an assortment** of **apricots, avocados, apples, and** grapes.

The **alluring** forest is **actually** near **a** city where it's **always** noisy **and always** loud.
The city is in the **ancient** heavens where **angels** dance in the **air** on **a** big, puffy cloud.

They sing **alleluias and** their songs **are astonishing and amazing**!
I love to watch them sing **and** dance while I **am** star gazing.

At any time, **angels are able** to **appear and** watch over us from the **attractive** bright sky.
When you look **above** ... you will be **awestruck** when you see them **all** dance, sing, **and** fly!

Our **Abba** Father **appoints** His **angels** to watch over us, making sure we **are** safe, **alive, and also** content.
Having His **adoring angels around** us **and alongside** us is **absolutely** heaven-sent!

Dear **Abba**,

As I **ask**, seek, **and** knock, you **are** there for me.
My prayers **are always answered** ... **abundantly**!

Thank you for making **animals**, bugs, **and army ants**.
Thank you for **all** the trees, shrubs, flowers, **and** plants.

Thank you for the **angels** ... they protect us **all** day long.
They **are attentive**, **angelic**, **astounding**, **and** strong!

Amen

Bb
BOB'S BUDDIES

I'm a **burly buck**-toothed **beaver** and my name is **Bob**.
I like to play **basketball** and eat corn on the cob.

I have a friend who is a **brown bear** and his name is **Blake**.
When I **bite** into my corn, he eats a **burnt, barbecued** steak.

Blake and I have a **buddy** named **Billy** who's a **busy bumblebee**.
He rides a **big, blue bus** to play **ball** with me.

He **buzzes** around … *bzzz, bzzz* … and **bravely** eats all the **butter** on my **boiled** cob of corn.
Sometimes, when he rides the **Boston** city **bus**, he **boldly beeps** the horn.

Beep, beep!

We also have a **buddy** who is a **black** and **brown bunny**.
He has **big, brown bunny** ears that **bend** so funny.

His name is **Benny** and we **barely** ever get **bored** …
because yesterday he **bought** a **brand**-new **Bronco** Ford.

While driving in **Benny's Bronco**, we chase **beautiful butterflies** that fly up and away.
Oh, how this makes for such a **bubbly, be-bopping,** and **bubbalicious** day!

By the way, did I mention that my **buddies** and I like to **bake**?
We love **baking batches** of **bountiful** pies and **blueberry** cake!

It's the **bumble-berry** pie that I especially love the **best** ...
but once it's in my **belly**, I need to **bounce** on my **bunk bed** for a **bit**
of a rest.

Another **buddy** I have is a **bald beetle bug** named **Blaine**.
We met **bouncing** a **basketball** outside in the rain.

Blaine thinks he's really **big**, **but** he's itty **bitty** and small.
I hope he doesn't get run over **by** a **bouncing basketball**!

Grandma **Bella** teaches **Blake**, **Billy**, **Benny**, **Blaine** and me about
Jesus every single day.
She reads her **Bible** to us, and teaches us **boys** how to love, **be** kind,
believe, and pray.

Grandma always keeps **bubblegum** in her **brightly** colored candy **bowl** ...
and when we **behave**, she **blesses** us with **baked banana bread** and a
brown Tootsie Roll!

I love my **beloved** grandma ... and I love my **buddies** too!
I **believe** Grandma **Bella**, **Blake**, **Billy**, **Benny**, and **Blaine** are the **best**
of the **best** ... don't you?

Bye for now and thanks for reading this story ...
our **brilliant** Lord gets all the praise and glory!

Cc
CAM'S CREATIONS

I'm a **clever, crawling caterpillar** … you **can call** me **Cam**.
My favorite thing to do is eat **cranberry** jam!

I like it on **cold** ice **cream cones** and on **cool, cut** bananas.
I even like it when I'm **cuddled** in my **cute, cozy** pajamas.

I like it on **Christmas cookies, coconut cupcakes**, and on **crumbly carrot cake**.
I especially like eating **cranberry** jam on my **curried Cajun** steak.

I like it on **caramels, candy canes, crackers**, and in **cups** of hot **creamy cocoa**.
I **could** even **consider** sharing my jam with my **colorful, calico cat**, Poco.

I'm kind of **curious** about **cooking** and **creating** new **canned cranberry** jam **combinations**.
I **could cover corn, cabbage, cantaloupe**, and **cooked cauliflower** to make **crispy** jam sensations.

I definitely know I **could** never eat **cranberry** jam on **cucumbers, capers, coleslaw**, or **cut**-up liver!
I must be a **coward** … 'cause **considering** that makes me **completely cringe** and shiver!

After all of these **crazy comments** on the foods that I **crave** most …
I only have the **courage** to **continue** eating **cranberry** jam on **crunchy, crusty** toast.

Can you tell me what **Christ** would do with **cranberry** jam and **crunchy, crusty** toast?
With **confidence**, He would feed it to the hungry … He is such a **calm, caring**, and **compassionate** host!

Dd
DESTINY DUCKS

My name is **Dickey Duckson** and I **dare** say, "I'm a **dazzling, dashing duck**."
I love to **doodle** and **draw**, read my **daily devotions**, and skate with a hockey puck.

I **do declare** that I am a **decent** and **dandy** cool **dude** …
and when I play hockey, I have never been **deliberately** booed.

Dallyn, **Don**, **Dave**, and **Darren** are my **dear ducky** friends.
When we have fun playing hockey, we hope the **day doesn't** end.

We waddle to the hockey rink, which is **down** a **dark** and **dirty** road each **day**.
We bring our skates, a **dollar**, and a **dime** when we **decide** to skate and play.

Our team is called the "**Destiny Ducks**" and we are **definitely dynamite!**
During our games, we **drop** the puck and play fair; we **dare** not ever fight.

We **dance**, waddle, and **dawdle** on the ice while we play.
It's a **divine** way to spend a **dreary** and **dull December day**.

After our game, **Daddy Duck drives** us to a **diner** for **desserts** and soft **drinks**.
It's just **down** a **dirt** road from our **dependable drop**-in hockey rink.

At the **diner**, the bakers **dish** out **dozens** of **Danish doughnuts** ...
dipped and **drizzled** with icing that tastes so sweet.
Their **delicious desserts** are such a **delightful** and **delectable** yummy
tasting treat!

Before we pay, we **dig deep** into our **dusty**, **denim** hockey bags for our
dollar and our **dime**.
This is how much these **Danish doughnuts** cost us every single time.

Can you believe this **dreamy, desirable doughnut deal**?
It's **definitely** better than any other **dinnertime** meal!

Dallyn, Don, Dave, Darren, and I will meet again next **December** with
our skates, **dollars, dimes**, and pucks,
because we are, no **doubt** about it ... the **determined, dedicated**, and
dynamite "Destiny Ducks!"

Ee
ERNIE AND BERNIE

Good **evening**,

I am an **enormous**, **easygoing elephant** and my name is **Ernie**.
I have an **enthusiastic** twin, and his name rhymes with mine, it's Bernie!

We look **exactly** alike and we **even** dress like **each** other.
It sure is fun and **entertaining** to have a twin brother!

Early each morning, Mama **Ella efficiently** makes us **eggs, éclairs** and toast.
Over-**easy eggs** is what we **especially enjoy eating** the most.

Mama **Ella encourages** us to **eat every** little crumb on our **extra**-large plate,
but we do have a wee problem, it is our **excessive elephant** weight.

Bernie and I have decided that we are going to **exercise each** and **every** day.
Well, **except** for on Sunday ... 'cause on this day, our **entire** family attends church to sing, learn, and, pray.

We start **each** day by touching our chubby **elephant elbows** to our chubby **elephant** knees.
Oh, this is not **easy**! I've really had **enough** ... let's move on, oh please, please, please!

Instead of taking the **elevator** or **escalator**, we now climb stairs until we
are **exhausted**, sweaty, and hot.
What gives us all this **energy**? Praying to Jesus our **Emmanuel** ... He helps
us out ... really ... a lot!

Eighteen days of **exercising** have gone by and Bernie and I feel **extremely**
healthy, **eager**, and **excellent** too.
We're also **excited** that we can now bend down to tie our **extra**-long
laces on our **extra**-large shoes! Whooo Hooooo!

Dear **Emmanuel**,

There is no **excuse** for Bernie and I not to **exercise** and for us not
to keep healthy and fit.
Please help us to always **encourage each** other so that we will
never, **ever** quit!

Ff
FLORA'S FRIENDS

My name is **Flora** and I'm a **female flounder fish** with lots and lots
of dots.
My scaly **fish fins** have **fifty-five** of these **flaky** little **freckles** and spots.

As a **flounder fish**, I've been **fortunate** to have **four fantastic friends**.
I'd love **for** you to hear about them again ... and again ... and again!

First of all, let me tell you about my **friend** who is a **frumpy frog**.
His name is **Frankie Finnigan** and he eats more than a **fully-fed** hog.

Frankie enjoys eating **French fries** and **flapjacks**, and when he's **finished**
all of that,
he says all this **feasting** makes him **feel fairly full** and **fairly fat**!

I also have a **furry friend** who is a **farm** dog named **Freddie**.
You would be so **fond** having him as your **favorite furry** teddy.

Freddie is such a **fine** and **funny fellow** with his **flip-floppy** ears.
Frankly, I think **floppy** ears would look **floppier** on a **fawn**—a baby deer.

Francesca is my **finicky flying friend** ... **for** she's a **feisty firefly**.
She **flitters** and **flutters fast**, **flying** real low and **flying** real high.

Another **fabulous friend** I have is a **field** cat named **Fluffy**.
Her **fancy face** is a ball of **fur** that is **fuzzy, fluffy,** and puffy.

Fluffy has **fat, furry feet** and a **fat** cat nose that continues to grow and

grow and grow!

Fortunately, her **fat** cat nose isn't growing **fast** ... it's growing **fairly** slow!

Dear Heavenly **Father**,

My **friends** will be my **friends** no matter how **frumpy, furry, funny, floppy, finicky, feisty, fancy,** or **fuzzy** they may be. **Frankie, Freddie, Francesca,** and **Fluffy** will **forever** be **faithful, favorable,** and **fascinating** to me!

Gg

GOOSEBERRY GUM

Good day!

I'm a **groovy gander goose** and my name is **Gloria Grace**.
I have **gorgeous gray goose** feathers all over my face.

I can blow really **grand** bubbles with my **gooey gooseberry gum** ...
and I like to **give** and share ... would you like to have some?

Look! I'll show you how **grand** I can **get** my bubble to **grow**.
I can **get** it to **grow** bigger than my **ghastly** big toe!

Oh! Oh! Pop **goes** my bubble and there **goes** my **gooey gum**!
Goodness gracious! It's stuck like **glue** onto my bum!

Help! Call the **governor**! **Get** mom and dad!
Gooey gum on my **goose** bum is making me sad.

I **guess** if I honk and **gasp**, the **gooey gum** will fall onto the **green, grassy ground**.
Or I could try flying and **gliding** around ... and around ... and around ... and around.

Oh, **gripes**, how am I ever **going** to **get** this **gooey gum** off so I can fly and play?
It's so **goofy** having this sticky, **gooey gum** on my **goosey** bum today.

I'm **grumpy, gloomy,** and **grouchy** ... I'm so sticky with **gooey gum**.
Oh, **good grief**, please … someone ... anyone ... **get** this off my bum!

Maybe if I **grin**, **giggle**, and wiggle, I can **gracefully get** this **glob** of **gooey gooseberry gum** to **gradually** fall.
Golly gosh, hopefully so 'cause soon I'm **golfing** with **Grandma** and **Grandpa** near the **Gander Grove** Mall.

Dear **Glorious God**,

Please **get** this **glob** of **gooey gooseberry gum** off my **goosey** bum today!
It's just so **gooey** and it's hard for me to fly south to relax, **golf**, and play.

God, I **gladly** promise to never again **get** my bubble to **grow** so **grand** and so high ...
because if I do, it could **go** "pop" onto my **gray goosey** cheek or my **gray goosey** thigh!

Hh
HANDSOME HARRY

Hello!
I'm a one **hundred**-year-old **hippo**, and my name is **Harry**.
Someday, I **honestly hope** to find love and marry.

Ha, **ha**, **ha**, **hippo**, **hip**, **hooray**!
How that would be a **happy**, **hippo** day!

I dream of marrying a **healthy hippopotamus** and **having** a wedding on top of the **hills**.
Just dreaming about it makes me **hungry** for **hot** dogs and gives me **hiccups**, **hay** fever, and chills.

I dream of **having** our **honeymoon** in **Hawaii**, where it's **humid**, **hot**, and sunny.
I can **hardly** wait to marry my **huge**, **hippo honey**!

I dream of us riding a **Harley** on the **hot**, **Hawaiian highways**.
Having her hold on tightly would make me **happy** … always.

My **heart** is aching to be a **handsome hippo husband**, but first I must find an **honorable** date.
Hmmmmm ... maybe **Henrietta** would be **honored** to be my **honey hippo** mate?

I dream of my **hippo** bride **having** wings and a **halo**, just like an angel above.
Oh, **Hallelujah**! **How heavenly** to be a **hippo** that's **happily** in love!

Holy Hosanna, **high** up in **heaven**,
forgive me, I'm not one **hundred** … I'm just *seven*!

With Your **healing hands**, please **help** me to be a **humble** and
honest hippo boy.
I pray for **honesty**, **happiness**, **harmony**, and **heaps** and **heaps**
of **hope** and joy.

Hugs,

Harry

Ii

ISAAC INGRAM

I live **in** the **interior** of **Israel**, and **I'm** an **intelligent iguana**.
I'd like for you to come and play with me … do you wanna?

Let me **introduce** myself … **I'm Isaac Ingram** and **I'm** ten years old.
Living **in Israel**, sure **is** hot … **it** barely ever gets **icy** and cold.

The **irresistible** sun can sure be hot and very **intense**,
but being an **iguana in** this heat just makes perfect sense!

As an **iguana, I** couldn't **imagine** living with the **Inuit in** their cold **igloos**
made of snow and **ice**.
Instead, I enjoy living **in Israel**, where **I** can **indulge in ice** cream and
instant minute rice!

Would you like **information** about **interesting** lands that are **indeed** far
away?
You and **I** could **investigate** these on the **internet** … come **inside**, what do
you say?

We could look up **international** countries such as **Iceland, Ireland, Israel,
Italy, India, Iraq,** and **Iran**.
Wow, when God had an **idea** to make all of these countries, He sure
invested in a plan!

He **invented** and created the **islands**, oceans, **icebergs**, sea, and land.
He also made you and **I** with His powerful and **ingenious** hand!

He did this all **in** just six days, and He says to rest on day seven.
How **incredible** that God made everything from His home **in** heaven!

It is only our **invisible** Heavenly Father who could **imagine** this life for
all **individuals** to enjoy—
a life made for everyone—**including** every **iguana**, man, woman, girl,
and boy.

Nothing **is impossible** with God; He **is** an **inspiration** to us all ...
and He **is instantly** there for you and **I**, whenever we need to call!

When you **invite** Jesus **into** your heart and every **inch** of the way ...
the Bible says to repent of your sins and to seek Him and pray.

Please don't **ignore** His **invitation** to you.
Indeed it will be a party! Whooo Hooooo!

Having an **intimate** relationship with Jesus **is** what God the Father, **intends**
for you and me.
His **important instructions** are **inscribed in** the Bible … an **influential**
book made for His whole family.

Jj
JAYDYN'S BIRTHDAY

I'm a **jolly**, **jumping jackrabbit** and my name is **Jaydyn James**.
It's **just** sooooo **jivey** having a "**J**" at the beginning of my names!

My brothers' names are **Jack**, **Jeremiah**, **Jimmy**, **Joe**, and **Josh**.
Wow, **jumping jeepers**, **jolly** golly, gosh!

My sisters' names start with a "**J**" as well ...
Jacqueline, **Joanna**, **Judy**, **Joan**, and **Janelle**.

My birthday starts with a "**J**" too; it's in the month of **June**.
Jumping jeepers, **jolly** golly, gosh ... it's going to be here soon!

I am sooooo excited to wear my **jazzy jacket** and **jeans** on my eleventh birthday.
I have one month to wait, 'cause **jumping jeepers**, **jolly** golly, gosh ...
it's already May!

I'm hoping to get a **journal**, **jigsaw** puzzle, car, **jet**, and **jeep**.
If I do, I would **joyfully** play without making a **jingle** sound or peep.

I would love it if you could **join** me in **June** for my very special day ...
it will be sooooo much **jolly** golly fun!
We'll **joke**, **jive**, **jump**, **jibber jabber**, and thank **Jesus** before eating **jars**
of **jellybeans** piled up high on a hot dog bun!

It is our **journey** with **Jesus** that is the very best gift that you and I could
ever receive.
Just pray to **Jehovah Jira**, and in Him, trust with **jolly** golly **joy**, and
always believe!

Kk

KIMBERLY KAY

I'm a **kind**, **koala** bear and my name is **Kimberly Kay**.
I love eating **ketchup** sandwiches every single day!

I had one for breakfast before my first day of school.
I think eating **ketchup** sandwiches is way too cool.

They make my tongue red and they also make me sneeze.
Oh! Oh! *Kerchoooooooo*! I need a **Kleenex**, please!

Today mama **koala** is in the **kitchen** making my lunch.
Do I ever love her a whole **kaboodle** bunch!

I have my very own lunch **kit**; can you guess what's inside?
Kidney beans, **kiwi**, a **Kit Kat** bar, and **Kentucky** chicken-fried.

Mama **Koala** packed a box of crayons too...
She even bought me my very own glue!

Keith and **Kyle** are my **kindergarten** friends and we love to have fun!
During recess we **kick** soccer balls … it's fun to **kick** and run!

Mr. **Kenny Kangaroo** is our teacher; he wears a Scottish **kilt** each day.
It looks like a colorful, patterned skirt … it's **kind** of cool, I'd say.

Dear **King** Jesus,

Thank you for my family, my **kindergarten** friends, and for
Mr. **Kenny Kangaroo**.
Thank you for my lunch **kit**, my crayons, and for my **Kraft**
tacky glue!

Keep us healthy and safe every single day
and **keep** your angels around us, this I pray.

Amen

Ll
LINDSEY'S LACES

My name is **Lindsey Lovelace**, and I'm a **lovely looking lioness**.
I **love** wearing **lime** colored **leotards** with my **long, lacy** dress.

I **love** being a **lioness**, and I thank the **Lord** for giving **life** to me!
I thank Him for making the **land, lakes, light,** and **lobsters** in the sea.

I also thank Him for **Leo** the **Lynx** and **Leah** the **Ladybug**.
They are my very best friends and we **love** to hug.

Leo, Leah and I **love** getting together to **laugh,** play, and to eat.
We **love** eating **lasagna** for **lunch** with **layers** of noodles and **lots** of meat.

Leo especially **loves** eating his **lunch**; he is the **lynx**,
but eating all this **lasagna** makes his breath … *stink*!

Leo uses **Listerine** mouthwash to make the **lingering** stink go away …
and then we get out our **Lego** blocks to build, share, and play!

I'd **love** to tell my friends about a problem that's hard to face.
I have not yet **learned** … how to tie my shoelace.

Last week, **Leo** and **Leah** showed me how to tie a bow and a **loose** knot,
but guess what? Not much **later** … I forgot!

Today at the **library**, I climbed a **ladder** to reach for a book on a shelf.
I read the **logical literature** on tying **laces** … all by myself!

I practiced for a **long** time, and I'll show you what I **learned**.
Look and **listen** carefully, **let** me show you, it's my turn.

I crossed the **left lace** over the right **lace**, and I pulled them together to make a knot and a **loop**.
Then, I ate **left**-over **lasagna** with **large ladles** of **lip**-smacking **lentil** bean soup.

Dear **Lord**,

I am thankful that **Leo**, **Leah** and I are written in the **Lamb**'s book of **life**…
and I am thankful that tying **long laces** doesn't give me **loads** of **long-lasting** strife.

Mm
MISS MARY

Good **morning**!

I'm a **mini mighty mouse** and **my** name is **Miss Mary**.
When **Mackenzie** and **Madi-Cat meet me** they act all **mean** and scary!

They **march** around **miserably** and **mob me** with a **musty** smelling **mop**.
My, oh **my**, oh **my**, oh **my**, this really **must** come to a stop!

A **mop** is so **mucky**, yucky, and **messy** and the smell **makes me** sick.
I'd rather be chased for **miles** and **miles** with **Mackenzie's** oven **mitt**.

I'm **much milder** than a **measly mosquito**, **moth**, **mule**, and **moose**.
Man, they need to **mellow** out and drink a **mug** of **mandarin mango** juice!

What I would like **most** is a bowl of **mushy macaroni** to **munch** on and eat.
Mmmm … **marshmallows** and a **maple milkshake** would be another **marvelous** treat!

I dream of **moving** into a **multi-million** dollar **mansion** and being a **mini mighty mouse** pet,
but if **Mackenzie** and **Madi**-Cat **meet me** again they would **mob me** with a **mop** and **miserably** fret!

Dear **Messiah**,

When I go to heaven, I hope to live in a **majestic mansion** that's **made** of cheese.
May I just ask for the **medium mozzarella**? **May** I, **may** I?
Please, please, please!

Nn

NASALLY NELLIE

My **name** is **Nellie** and I'm a **nasally nanny** goat with a face that's blotchy and red.
For **nine** days **now**, I've been wearing my **nightgown** while sick in my bed.

I've been reading the **New** Testament and the **national newspapers** too.
This is all I can do when I'm sick with this **nasally** cold and flu.

During the day, I **nibble** on **nectarines**, slurp **noodle** soup, and then **nod** off to **nap**.
I have **numbers** of teddy bears **nestled** high in my bed and on top of my lap.

It's **not** a **nice** feeling to be **nauseous**, **nasally**, sad, and sick ...
and so at **noon**, my mama is taking me to see my doctor ... Dr. **Nick**.

Dr. **Nick's nickname** is Dr. **Nosebump** because he has a **noticeable** bump on the end of his long, **narrow nose**.
I'm sorry if I sound **negative**, but I wonder if these bumps are also **next** to his **not**-so-**nice**-looking toes.

Dr. **Nosebump** is a very **nice** man, and **Nurse Nancy** is very **nice** too.
They help me get better when I'm sick with this **nasty** cold and flu.

The best medicine of all is praying to Jesus of **Nazareth** who lives in the heavens above.
He is full of **niceness**, peace, healing, strength, and lots and lots of **nurturing** love.

Jesus is always **nearby** and **nodding** with a smile as we **noisily** sing **notes**, dance, and jump.
Thank you Jesus, **Nurse Nancy**, and thank you to my doctor ....
Dr. **Nosebump**!

Oo

OLLIE OCTOPUS

I'm an **ordinary octopus** and my name is **Oliver**, but I get called **Ollie**.
Dreaming about being in the Winter **Olympics** makes me feel **oh** so jolly!

I dream **of** my **octopus** friends and I riding **outdoors** in an **orange** colored luge.
Oh my ... I wonder if we'd fit ... we're just a bit **overweight**, just a bit too huge.

Maybe **Ozzie**, **Owen**, **Olivia**, and I would fit if we sucked in **our** bellies and held **our** breath tight.
I'm sure that four squashed **octopus** friends would be an **odd** and **outrageous** sight!

Riding a luge in the **Olympics** would be **oodles** and **oodles of** fun!
On our days **off** we could fly **overseas** and relax **outside** in the sun.

The **Orient** is an **outlandish** place where I have always wanted to go.
We couldn't bring **our** luge though ... they haven't an **ounce of** snow!

Digging for **oysters** and **organic** clams by the **ocean** shore is something I'd like to do.
I **often** wonder what **one** would taste like … I really haven't a clue.

In my **opinion**, **oysters** would have an **overwhelming odor** and would be really smelly.
I definitely don't want smelly, **oily oysters** going into my **octopus** belly!

When I eat **oatmeal once** a day, I feel **outstanding**, healthy, and **overly** strong.
Riding a luge for an **Olympic** team is where I know I **ought** to belong.

Sometime after **October**, when the Winter **Olympics** is **on** everyone's TV...
only cheer for the **octopus** team. We'll do more than **okay** … you'll see!

Dear **omniscient** Lord,

I'm **overjoyed** with the **opportunities** that You have given to me.
Please help me to remain **open** and **obedient** … so happy I will be!

Pp
PRINCESS PAT

I'm a **pretty**, **pink pig** and my name is **Princess Pat**.
I look quite **porky**, **pudgy**, and fat.

My favorite **past** time is to eat and eat and eat …
I eat everything except **pork** chops and **pigs**' feet!

My favorite foods all start with the letter "P" … **pie**, **porridge**, **pretzels**,
and **pop**.
Oh **please**, I **positively** cannot stop!

I love eating **pancakes**, **potatoes**, **peanuts**, **pudding**, **purple popsicles**,
pasta, **perogies**, **peppermints**, **pepperoni pizza**, and **popcorn** too.
I even **pack piles** of sour **pickles** into my **pocket**, and I'd like to **patiently**
pass them onto you … and you … and you!

Being a **porky pig** is just **plain** ol' fun …
but, eating all this food makes me **practically** weigh a ton!

Some days I **pretend** to **put** myself on a **poultry** diet…
but, **pigging** out in my **pigpen** can sure be a riot!

Perhaps if I **plan** to eat **peaches**, **pomegranates**, **peas**, **pineapples**,
papaya, **parsnips**, **pumpkin**, **plums**, **peppers**, **prunes**, and **poached**
pears from a **plate**, **pail** or tin …
then it's **probably possible** that someday I'll be looking less **plump**, and
a little more thin.

I **praise** the **powerful Prince** of **Peace** for making all the **pleasant** foods that start with the letter "**P**."
I also **praise** Him for making **precious people** like you, and **porky pigs** like me!

Qq

QUINTON THE QUAIL

My name is **Quinton** and I'm a **quaint** little **quail**.
I have lots of brown feathers on my short, bird tail.

I'm a **quiet** little **quail** and I chirp, I do not **quack**.
Actually, only a **quacking** duck is good at that.

I live near a porcupine named **Quincy** ... and does he ever have long,
sharp **quills**!
It sure makes me **queasy** to think of one getting stuck in my
bird bill!

Never **quarrel** with a porcupine ... you never know where his **quills**
could poke.
I am not kidding ... this is not a **quirky** joke!

My **quiet** little **quail** home is high up in a tree.
I even have a **quilt** up there ... would you like to see?

Mama **Quail** made my **quilt** so when I'm **quivering**, I'll be warm,
snug, and cozy.
Sometimes, **Quincy quickly** and **quietly** sneaks up to see it ... he's
just so nosy.

My nest is near a swarm of honeybees and they sure like to buzz.
Their wee little bodies are covered in **quantities** of black and yellow fuzz.

The **queen** bees are the boss, and they make sure their bees make **quality** honey.
Without **question**, it does taste delicious whether it's hard or runny!

It's now **quite** easy to get **quarts** of honey for my toast and tea.
It sure is convenient having a neighbor who is a busy honeybee!

Thank you God, for making **quails**, porcupines, honey bees, and **queen** bees.
Your **quality** creation is so precious and dear to my friends and to me!

Rr
ROBBY'S STEW

I am a **radiant**, **red robin** and my name is **Robby** Brewster.
My **reliable** neighbor is a **robust** cock-a-doodling **rooster**.

His name is **Rusty**, and he is **really**, **really**, cool.
We often **refresh** and **relax** in his **rectangular** pool.

Rusty and I like **rummaging** for worms near a **roaring river** each day.
After it **rains**, the worms **roam** on the **rocks**, but I'm **really** sorry to say ...

we **race** to catch them 'cause they taste **remarkable** in our stew.
In fact, I've **read** that **roasted** worm stew is **reasonably** good for you!

The worms are **remotely** slimy and **rather** quite tasty and yummy.
They are so **replenishing** going into my **round, rumbling** tummy!

I **reckon** you'd like to **receive** our **rare** and **rustic recipe** for "roasted
worm stew."
It has a few **raw radishes**, but you can get **rid** of them if you **really**
want to!

The worms **resemble** spaghetti noodles ... unlike **ravioli**, they are **rubbery**,
long and sticky.
Oh, you **really** should **request** some ... let's not be **rude** and picky!

Just **remember**, if your **refrigerator remains** empty and bare,
rush on over to my place, I am always **ready** to give and share!

Reading God's word with **roasted** worms in my belly is simply the best ...
especially when I'm **resting** and **reclining** in my **refurbished robin** nest!

This story is not a **ridiculous rumor** or **rhyme** ... it **really** is the best
roasted worm stew!
So, plug your nose **really, really**, tight 'cause the **ripe** and **rank** smell is
repulsive ... PeeeeeeU!

Ss

SPAGHETTI SQUASH

I'm a **sincere, silly swan** and my name is **Sue**.
Sunday I cooked **spaghetti squash** for **supper**, but it **smelled** like **stinky** glue!

It was **slimy** and **sticky** and really quite **soggy, slippery, squishy**, and gooey.
Somehow I **seemed** to have **simmered** and **stirred** it too long ... oh, phooey!

So now I have **stinky, slimy, sticky, soggy, slippery, squishy**, and gooey **spaghetti squash stuck** inside my belly!
I would've been **satisfied** if I had just **swallowed soup, salad, sliced sausages**, and a **sandwich** made with **strawberry** jelly.

Some sociable swans seriously suggest that **slowly slurping several sips** of **sweet soda** will **soften** it all up.
I **suppose** I'll try this ... please **send** me a **straw** and a **sterling silver saucer** with a **sterling silver** cup.

Surprisingly, slurping down a **smidge** of **sweet soda** was **splendid** and nice.
It felt **smooth** as **silk** ... **sliding** down with **several scoops** of **square-shaped** ice.

The next time I cook **spaghetti squash**, I hope it won't **smell** and taste like **stinky, slimy, sticky, soggy, slippery, squishy**, and gooey glue!
Instead, I'll **see** if **Sydney**, my **super-smart sister**, will cook and **serve** it … she **seems** to always know what to do!

Sydney says the **secret** to cooking **scrumptious spaghetti squash** is really quite **simple** and really quite a cinch.
When she **seasons** it with **spices, salt**, and **small sesame seeds**, she **sparingly sprinkles** a pinch.

Dear **Savior**,

Thank you for creating **spaghetti squash**, 'cause when it's cooked right, it is **splendidly** yummy!
It **simply smells** and tastes **superb** when it's **settling** down into my **sleek** and **slender** tummy!

Sincerely,

Sally Sue

Tt
TRIPLET TURKEYS

My name is **Tammy** ...
and my brother's names are **Timmy** and **Tommy**.

We are **triplet turkeys** and we live in a honky **tonk town** in
southern **Tennessee**.
We **talk** with a **twangy** accent … can you unnnderrrrstannnnnd me?

Today is **Tuesday** and we're meeting at my **table** for **toast, tarts,** and **tasty
Tetley tea**.
How about y'all **try to** come join my brothers and me?

Our friend, **Ted** the **toad** will be stopping on by ... he's a **two** year old
toddler, just a **tiny tot**.
We **tend to** play **tag** when the **temperature's too** hot.

Titus the **tiger** is our friend **too** and he is also coming **to** my house.
He doesn't **talk** much ... he's **tame** and **timid** like a **teensy**-weensy mouse.

Myrtle the **turtle** is slooooowly **trotting** on her way …
it could **take** some **time** before she gets here **to** play.

Tick tock, tick tock, is Myrtle here yet?
Someone get her on a jet!

Once she finally gets here, Myrtle the **turtle** likes **to tease** and **tickle** my
tiny turkey toes.
When she does, **Timmy, Tommy,** and I **try to tip toe** and **tag** her with a
ten-foot water hose!

(Read with a **Tennessee Twang**)

Together we always have **tons** and **tons** of fun …
but when we have a water fight, we run, run, run!

Even Myrtle the **turtle tries to** pick up her pace.
Someone, **time** her, this is a **time-ticking** race!

My brothers and I sure have fun with all of our **terrific** friends ...
and when it comes **to** water fights, we would **totally** do it again!

Taking time to worship and **to turn** our hearts **to** Jesus is **truly**
important **to Timmy**, **Tommy**, and I.
He **teaches** us how **to** love and **trust** ... Oh how I love that guy!

The word of God also **tells** us **to** worship and obey ...
and how important it is **to** forgive and **to** pray.

Tootlelooo for now,
Let's **take** a bow.

Gobble, gobble. **Teeeeheeeeheeee!**
It's **time** for more **toast**, **tarts**, and **tasty Tetley tea!**

Uu
URSULA THE UNICORN

My name is **Ursula** and I am a **unicorn** ... I am not a horse.
Some may think I am make-believe, but I am not–of course!

I am written about in **unique** and **unforgettable** books.
Why don't you open them **up** and take a little look?

Sometimes my picture is painted on **umbrellas** for little girls and little boys ...
and sometimes I may be peeking **under** all your books and **under** all your toys.

Uh, oh! When you look in your **untidy** chest of drawers, I can be **uncovered** there.
Unbelievable as it sounds ... I can **usually** be found almost anywhere!

Unlike horses, you may dream of me riding a **unicycle** while you **unconsciously** sleep.
Or you may dream of me flying high into the **universe** without **uttering** a neigh or a peep.

Sometimes I just fly **under** clouds and leap **up,** **Up** and around.
I jump **ultra**-high and twirl **until** my feet touch the ground.

Untold stories are written about **us** in Old Testament books.
Please open **up** your **useful** Bible and take a little look.

Did you know that **unicorns** had horns that were **unusually** strong?
They were also very straight and also very long.

Please know and **understand** the word of God is not just a
book and it's not just a story.
Our **ultimate** Lord teaches **us** how to live and **unite** …
He gets all the **unconditional** glory!

Numbers 23:22 (KJV) "God brought them out of Egypt; he hath as it were the strength of a **unicorn**."

Vv
VICKI'S VISIT

I'm a **very vocal vixen** and my name is **Vicki Voll**.
I live in a **valley** and down a foxhole.

In the **valley** also lives **venomous vipers** that are hidden under rocks.
Can you guess which animal I am? I am a female fox.

The **valley** is near **Vermont** where I live with my cousins **Vince**, **Vic**, and **Vance**.
We all enjoy singing and we sure love to dance, dance, dance!

Today Aunt **Vera** will be taking us in her **Volkswagen Van** to **visit** Grandma **Veronica**.
Our grandma is **very**, **very** good at singing and playing her harmonica.

She plays the **violin** too and she's **very** good at that …
and while she plays, she wears a silly **velvet** hat!

Grandma has a **vibrato voice** and she plays and sings every **version** of all the Bible songs.
She always reminds us to eat our **veggies**, take our **vitamins**, and to dance and sing along!

She sings **verses** while she **vacuums**, and she plays her **violin** while worshiping the Lord.
As you can see, Grandma **Veronica virtually** never ever gets tired or bored.

She sings and plays with lots of **victory**, **vim**, and **vigor**.
I pray that I'll be like my grandma when I get bigger.

She has **volumes** of tight curly hair and it's **violet** too.
I really like her **violet** colored hair … don't you?

Grandma **Veronica** lives in a **village** down by a river, in a house with a
view near the **valley**.
She **volunteers** her time, knitting **vests** and **versatile** sweaters with her
virtuous friend **Valerie**.

She buys her yarn and needles at **Value Village**, as she **vows** this is the
very best store in town.
She **ventures** there to buy her yarn with a **voucher** in a **variety** of shades
of beige and brown.

Grandma's **vision** isn't all that great …
so she buys her glasses at a **valued** discount rate.

I can **vent**, **verify**, and **verbally** say that grandma made a **vest** for me with
lots of **vertical** lines and **visible** dots …
and I can **vent**, **verify**, and **verbally** say that I sure love my Grandma
Veronica lots and lots and lots!

Ww
WINKY WILBUR

My name is **Winky Wilbur** and I'm a fuzzy **wuzzy worm**.
My hair is **wonderfully wavy** ... and it looks like a perm!

I live in the **wilderness** beside Mr. **Warricks**' place.
He's a **wise** old man **with white whiskers** on his face.

Mr. **Warrick** is planting and **watering** his garden **Wednesday**
morning.
I'll just **watch** out my **window** 'cause **working** in **windy weather**
seems **way** too boring.

Mr. **Warrick** has a **wagon** full of dirt, tools, and seeds.
He'll be planting fruits and veggies ... foods he **wants** and needs.

The **wheels** on his **wagon** are **white** and black ...
and the seeds by his **wagon** are in a great big sack.

Wow! There's a lot of **weeds** that Mr. **Warrick will** have to pick so
his garden **will** grow!
I **wonder** if he **will want** help digging **weeds with** his pitch fork, shovel,
and hoe.

Mr. **Warrick will** be planting and **watering wheat** grass, **watermelon**,
watercress, and some **walnut** trees.
Oh boy, I'll have to **watch** out for all those **wacky-winged wasps** and
wacky-winged bees!

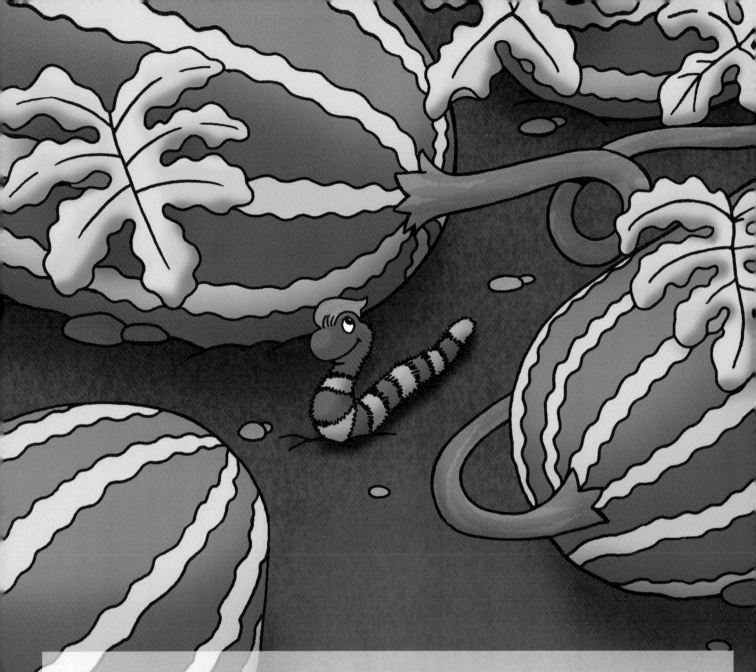

Wouldn't it be **wonderful** if **waffles** topped **with whipped** cream **would** grow in a garden?
Hmmmmm ... I **wonder** if they **would wilt** and I **wonder** if they **would** harden.

While I **wiggle**, **whistle**, and **worship** God in the garden all **week** long ...
I'll help keep Mr. **Warricks'** plants healthy, **well**, and strong!

Soon the **wheat** grass, **watercress**, and **walnuts will** be **washed** and taste oh so **wonderfully** yummy ...
but it's the red, juicy **watermelon** that I can't **wait** to put into my fuzzy **wuzzy** tummy!

Xx
CHICKEN POX

My name is **Xavier** and I'm a sly **fox**.
Today I woke up with the chicken **pox**!

I have itchy, red **pox** from the top of my head to the tips of my toes.
I even have **extra pox** all around my whiskers and nose!

Mama **Fox** says that T-**Rex** is covered with itchy **pox** too.
I wonder ... could my dino buddy have this chicken **pox** flu?

I pray these itchy **pox** will soon go away!
Would you recommend I get an **X-ray**?

Should I be **examined** by Dr. **Lox**?
Is it possible that he can **fix** chicken **pox**?

Chicken **pox**, chicken **pox** *gooooo* away!
I do not want you bothering me today!

I itch and I scratch and these **pox** make me spotty.
I have **maximum** dots on my head and my body!

Today, I have an appointment to visit Dr. **Lox**.
Mama **Fox** says that he can **fix** chicken **pox**.

Dr. **Lox** has **mixed** an **excellent** lotion to put all over my itchy red **pox**.
He says I just need to **relax** and keep warm with my feet in my socks.

The **expensive** lotion is made in a **box** with herbs, **flax**, and sticks.
Without question … it is an **extraordinary** chicken **pox mix**!

In **exactly six** days, I'll be **excited** to look at myself in the mirror …
because thanks to Jesus and Dr. **Lox**, the **pox** will soon disappear!

Yy

YODELING YANNI

My name is **Yanni** and I'm a **yippy**, **yappy yak**.
Yesterday, after I **yawned**, I ate **yellow yogurt** for my snack.

The flavor was banana and it tasted **yummy** and sweet.
Yum, **yum** … banana **yogurt** is now my favorite treat!

Yesterday, after I **yawned**, I bought a **yo-yo** at the local store.
I wanted to buy **yellow yams** too, but they didn't have any more.

Yahoo, Yippee Yippee Yay!
I am just soooo excited to say …

I bought the last **yo-yo** and the color is **yellow**.
It moves up and down like a bowl full of Jell-O!

Yesterday, after I **yawned**, I played with my **yo-yo**, and I tried making one too.
All I needed was **yellow yarn**, a spool, and a dab of white craft glue.

I **yanked** the **yellow yarn** around and around an empty spool of thread …
then I hid my **yellow yo-yo** in a **yellow** box that's underneath my snuggly bed.

Yesterday, after I **yawned**, I **yodeled** in my **yard** and over the rolling hills.
The sound of **yodeling** makes me **yippy** and **yappy** and gives me the chills!

Yes! I love being a **young yak** … it's fun being me!
Just love **yourself** too, and happy **you'll** be!

Thank **you Yahweh** God for the fun I had this **year**.
When I **yodel** to **You**, I feel **Your** presence near!

Zz
ZALTON ZOO

I am a **zippy**, **zingy zebra**, and my name is **Zack**.
I have black and white stripes going up and down my back.

I live in a home at the **Zalton Zoo** …
and my best friend, **Zane**, is a **zany** kangaroo.

Zane always wears his kangaroo sweater …
but I like my **zebra** jacket much better!

My **zebra** jacket has a **zipper** instead of buttons, a hood, and a kangaroo pouch.
It's nice to cozy up with when I'm eating fried **zucchini** on my polka-dotted couch.

My neighbor, **Zeke**, is a pig and he is full of **zest** and **zeal**.
He rolls and rolls in the mud like a wagon wheel.

He's a lazy, crazy pig and he's very large and smelly.
He walks real slow 'cause he has a huge potbelly.

Zeke watches visitors **zigzag** around as they look at us all.
It makes him feel **zippy** and **zappy** and big and tall.

The tallest animal at the **zoo** is a giraffe named **Zorro**.
She'll be having her baby calf sometime tomorrow!

You'll also meet **Zoë** the elephant when you come to the **zoo**.
She came here from **Zimbabwe** when she was just two.

So please, come **zoom** on by the **Zalton Zoo** ...
all of us **zany** and **zingy** animals would love to welcome you!

More importantly, it is God the Father who would love to welcome
you into His Kingdom of **Zion**.
Just ask his son, Jesus Christ, into your heart, for it is Him you can
always rely on.

CPSIA information can be obtained
at www.ICGtesting.com
Printed in the USA
LVIW022124211012

303578LV00005BA

9 781467 035323